FRANKIE'S
MAGIC
FOOTBALL

D0581214

BY FRANK LAMPARD

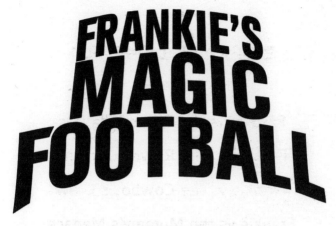

FRANKIE'S MAGIC FOOTBALL

THE GRIZZLY GAMES

FRANK LAMPARD

LITTLE, BROWN BOOKS FOR YOUNG READERS
www.lbkids.co.uk

LITTLE, BROWN BOOKS FOR YOUNG READERS

First published in Great Britain in 2015 by Hodder & Stoughton

1 3 5 7 9 10 8 6 4 2

Copyright © 2015 by Lamps On Productions

The moral right of the author has been asserted.

A CIP catalogue record for this book
is available from the British Library.

ISBN 978-0-349132-0-51

Typeset in Cantarell by M Rules
Printed and bound in Great Britain by
Clays Ltd, St Ives plc

The paper and board used in this book are
made from wood from responsible sources.

MIX
Paper from
responsible sources
FSC® C104740

Little, Brown Books for Young Readers
An imprint of
Hachette Children's Group
Part of Hodder & Stoughton
Carmelite House
50 Victoria Embankment
London EC4Y 0DZ

An Hachette UK Company
www.hachette.co.uk

www.lbkids.co.uk

*To my mum Pat, who encouraged
me to do my homework in between
kicking a ball all around the house,
and is still with me every
step of the way.*

Welcome to a fantastic Fantasy League – the greatest football competition ever held in this world or any other!

You'll need four on a team, so choose carefully. This is a lot more serious than a game in the park. You'll never know who your next opponents will be, or where you'll face them.

So lace up your boots, players, and good luck! The whistle's about to blow!

The Ref

PART ONE

CHAPTER 1

Mr Donald stood at the front of
the class. "This week we're doing a
special project," he announced.

Frankie grinned. As well as
being their teacher, Mr Donald was
the football coach at school. His
projects usually had something to
do with football.

Mr Donald reached into his desk and pulled out a piece of material. As he unrolled it, Frankie realized it was a flag with two red blocks either side of a white block. In the middle was a red leaf.

"Does anyone recognize this?" their teacher asked, holding the flag up above his head.

Louise's hand shot up. "It's the Canadian flag, sir!" she said. Louise was *really* clever.

Mr Donald nodded. "That's right, Louise. And who can tell me something about Canada?"

Louise's hand went up again,

but so did several others. Charlie
raised his arm slowly and the class
giggled. As usual, he was wearing
his goalie gloves. Mr Donald let him
keep them on all the time, because
he knew how much football meant
to Charlie. All the teachers at
school did.

"Yes, Charles?" said Mr Donald.

"It's in the United States, sir!" said Charlie.

Mr Donald frowned. "Close ..." he said.

Louise's hand waved frantically. "Sir, it's in North America, but not the USA. It's where the Women's World Cup is being held this summer!"

"Exactly!" said Mr Donald. "Which makes it the perfect subject for our project."

For the next half hour, their teacher told them all about Canada. Apparently it was nearly forty times bigger than the United Kingdom, but only had half as many people. Mr Donald pinned a map to the board, and pointed out enormous mountain ranges and lakes. The northern parts reached the Arctic Circle and were covered in snow and ice.

"You can see huge whales swimming off the coast, and in the winter polar bears come into the villages looking for food!" their teacher said. "They have brown bears, too — they're called grizzlies."

Frankie listened, fascinated. "I've always wanted to see a bear in the wild," he said.

"I'm not sure you'd want to meet a Canadian grizzly," said Mr Donald, laughing. Then he folded his arms and stared at Frankie. "They can be pretty dangerous. What would you do?"

"I'd run fast!" said Frankie.

Mr Donald shook his head. "Not a good idea," he said. "Bears can easily outrun a person."

"I'd climb a tree!" said Charlie.

"Nope," said their teacher. "Bears can climb too. The best idea is to throw some food, or something else to distract them, then walk away slowly facing them. If they do get close, stretch out your arms and shout loudly. Pretend to be big!"

The bell went, and everyone started to put away their books. "After break, we'll talk more about the history of Canada and the sort of animals that live there," said Mr Donald.

As they filed out of the classroom, Louise paused by his desk.

"So why is there a leaf on their flag?" she asked.

"Good question," said Mr Donald. "It's a maple leaf, and it's the national symbol of Canada. Maple trees grow in lots of countries though — this one included. In fact, there's a tree in the school grounds, by the sports pavilion."

Frankie and the rest of the class put on their coats and went outside. A light drizzle was falling and puddles dotted the playground. Frankie took his school bag with him, because it contained the magic football. The football opened up portals to all sorts of adventures, and he didn't want to it to fall into the wrong hands.

"I hope I play in the Women's World Cup one day," said Louise.

Frankie placed a hand on her

shoulder. "You will one day, Lou, for sure!"

"Dream on," said a voice. Frankie turned around and saw his brother Kevin and his friends in their football kit. They were obviously coming back from a PE lesson.

"Go away, Kev," said Charlie. "Louise is better than you any day."

Kevin blushed and his friends snorted.

"She's just a girl!" he said. "Girls shouldn't even be allowed a World Cup. What a waste of time!"

Frankie knew that his brother could be an idiot sometimes, but this was worse than usual. "Ignore him, Lou," Frankie whispered to his friend.

But as he turned around, Frankie felt his bag straps snag. Kevin was trying to tug it off his shoulders.

"Hey, get off!" said Frankie.

Kevin rummaged inside the bag, ignoring him. Before Frankie could stop him, he'd grasped the magic football and pulled it out. Kevin glanced round at his friends, a smirk playing across his lips. "Do you guys fancy one more game?" he asked, winking. "We can teach this lot a lesson!"

Frankie swallowed nervously.

"Seriously, Kev, you don't want to play with that," he said.

Kevin's eyes twinkled mischievously. He knew the power of the magic football, because he'd followed Frankie on adventures in the past.

"Don't I?" he said.

For a few seconds they stared at each other, then Kevin's eyes narrowed at something beyond Frankie. Mr Donald was walking across the car park, carrying a stack of folders so tall that he couldn't see over the top.

"OK – here you go," said Kevin. He held out the ball to Frankie. But

as Frankie reached out for it, Kevin
dropped the ball, then swung his
foot at it.

Charlie leaped as the football
shot over all their heads, right
towards the car park.

"Look out, sir!" cried Louise.

Mr Donald jumped at the
warning, twisting round, but it was
too late. The ball bounced right into
his folders, knocking them out of
his hands.

"Quick, let's get out of here!"
Frankie heard one of Kevin's friends
say. Their feet pounded away.

Frankie couldn't take his eyes
off Mr Donald. His teacher's face

had gone the colour of beetroot. "Frankie!" he shouted. "Come here, now."

"Donaldo looks mad!" said Charlie. "You should tell him the truth — it was Kevin's fault."

With feet as heavy as lead, Frankie and his friends trooped towards Mr Donald, who was picking up all the folders.

"What's the meaning of this?" he said. "You know you're not allowed to play football beside the car park. It's very dangerous."

Charlie and Louise were glaring at Frankie. *Tell him!* mouthed Louise.

"I'm sorry, sir," said Frankie, ignoring her. "It won't happen again."

Mr Donald's nostrils flared. "Make sure it doesn't," he said, before striding off.

Frankie and his friends watched them go.

"Why didn't you tell the truth?" asked Louise.

"Because my parents had a letter," said Frankie. "If Kevin gets into any more trouble, he'll be suspended."

"He'd deserve it," grumbled Charlie. He looked around. "Anyway, where's the football?"

Frankie scanned the car park, wandering back and forth. "It must have landed somewhere around here," he muttered. Then, between two cars, he saw a shimmering puddle on the ground. It didn't look like any ordinary puddle, with that sparkling light. "Oh no . . ." he said, guessing what had happened.

The others joined him.

"A portal!" said Louise, reading Frankie's thoughts. "Where does it go to?"

Frankie checked his watch. Five minutes until break ended. "There's only one way to find out!" he said,

looking around at the others.
"Ready for another trip?"

His friends grinned. "I'm always ready," said Charlie.

"Let's do it!" said Louise.

Together they jumped into the air and fell, with a splash of sparkling water, into the puddle . . .

CHAPTER 2

Only they didn't stop falling. They plunged down and down into freezing cold water. All around Frankie saw bubbles as Charlie and Louise struggled in the water beside him.

We'll turn into ice cubes down here! he thought, trying not to panic.

Frankie kicked, and pushed up through the water. As his head broke the surface, he sucked in a deep breath and gasped.

The car park had gone, and they weren't in a puddle. Frankie found himself in the middle of a crystal-clear lake, surrounded by huge mountains. Snow capped the tallest peaks. At the lake's edge were a few log cabins with small rowing boats tied up. Though the sun beat down from a clear blue sky, warming his face, Frankie shivered. Louise and Charlie bobbed beside him, treading water.

"Is everyone OK?" he asked. The

other two nodded, but their teeth
were chattering. "Let's swim to
shore," said Frankie.

He set off, but it was hard going.
His limbs felt numb and his clothes
weighed him down. However, soon
he felt pebbles beneath his feet. He
dragged himself the last few metres

to the lake's edge. Then he turned to offer his hands to Charlie and Louise.

"Where are we?" asked Charlie, puffing.

Louise brushed her wet hair out of her eyes and gazed up at the mountains. "I don't know," she said, "but it's incredible!"

Something splashed in the middle of the lake, and a head broke the surface. "Help!" barked a familiar voice.

Frankie's heart leapt. "It's Max!"

His little dog was wriggling his paws to stay afloat, but he'd never been much of a swimmer.

I should have known the magic football would bring him, too!

Frankie rushed back to the water's edge and began to wade in, when a huge shape bounded along one of the jetties and leapt into the water, throwing up a wave. It was a huge black dog, its broad muzzle rising above the surface as it began swimming towards Max. A girl ran along the jetty as well.

"Go, Claude!" she shouted.

Max let out a yelp and his little head sank beneath the water.

"Oh no!" cried Charlie. "Max is drowning!" As the words left his mouth, the massive dog dove beneath the water and disappeared. Frankie counted under his breath. *One, two* ... On the count of three, the dog burst through the surface of the water, dangling a very soggy Max in his jaws.

"Let me go!" said Max, struggling.

The black dog ignored him and turned back towards the shore, carrying Max all the way. Finally, he dropped him on the bank near the jetty. Max shook his coat violently, throwing off a spray of water droplets. Frankie and his friends ran around the lake's edge to join the girl and the two dogs. Close up, Frankie realised she was only a year or two older than them, but taller than even his brother Kevin. She had short fair hair, and lots of freckles.

"Thank you!" said Frankie. "You saved my dog."

The girl smiled. "Don't thank me — thank Claude," she said.

Frankie looked at her dog. His head came up to Frankie's shoulder, and he had a droopy mouth with large, sad-looking eyes.

"Thank you, Claude," said Frankie. Max gave a low grumble, turning up his snout. "I think you've hurt his pride, though." Normally, Frankie's dog could talk when they went through magical portals. Frankie guessed he was being careful not to talk in front of this girl in case it led to some difficult questions.

"You guys are tough swimming in water this cold!" said the girl. "Though maybe it was too much for your little dog." Max let out another growl at the word "little". Fortunately the girl didn't seem to notice. "My name's Danni," she said. She pointed to the cabin next to them. "I live here."

"I'm Frankie, and these are my friends Louise and Charlie," said Frankie. "The dog's called Max."

"Claude's an amazing swimmer," said Louise.

"He's a Newfie," Danni said. "They have webbed paws."

"Sounds more like a fish to me," muttered Max.

Frankie shushed him. He didn't want to alarm the girl who'd helped them.

"What's a Newfie?" said Charlie.

"It's short for Newfoundland," said Danni, patting Claude's side. "That's the island where the breed came from originally."

I know that name from somewhere, thought Frankie. Then he remembered – the map

Mr Donald had shown them that morning.

"Newfoundland is in Canada!" he said.

Danni frowned. "Uh, yeah! We're in Canada," she said. "Though we're nowhere near Newfoundland." She gave them an odd look.

Frankie gazed at the magnificent mountains. *These must be the Rockies!* "Er ... yeah. Right," he said. "We knew that!"

"We're on holiday," added Louise.

"In Vancouver, I guess," said Danni, raising an eyebrow.

"Yes," said Frankie.

The girl looked at Charlie's gloves. "So, you're a goalkeeper. Me too!"

"Best in the county!" said Frankie.

Charlie blushed. "If you say so," he mumbled.

"Do you play on a team?" asked Louise.

Danni nodded. "We have a tournament later today — all the girls' teams from the local area. It's like a mini World Cup! Hey, why don't you come and watch?"

"We'd love to!" said Louise.

"Cool, just wait here while I get my things from inside," said

Danni. She paused and turned back, inspecting their dripping clothes. "Do you want to get changed?"

Frankie shook his head. If they were suddenly transported back to school, he'd have no way of returning any clothes they borrowed.

"Don't worry about us," he said, trying not to shiver. "We'll dry out in no time."

Claude stayed outside next to them. Max trotted up to him, and sniffed. "OK, so you're a good swimmer, big guy, but I bet you're no good at chasing squirrels."

The Newfie cocked his head, obviously confused.

"I can't believe we're in Canada!" said Louise. "It must be because we were studying it earlier."

Frankie breathed in the cool mountain air. "Yes, but what do you think we're here to do? Normally the magic football sets us some sort of challenge, or wants us to help someone."

"Danni doesn't seem to need our help," said Charlie. "In fact, it was her dog that rescued Max!"

"I didn't need rescuing," said Max. "I was enjoying a paddle."

Frankie crouched and stroked him behind his damp ears. "Whatever you say, boy."

A moment later, Danni emerged with a sports bag over her shoulder. "Let's go!"

Suddenly, Claude gave a deep bark and padded back to the water's edge. "What's he found now?" said Danni, peering over the lake. "There's something bobbing out there."

Sure enough, Frankie saw it too. "My football!" he said. But it was too late – the battered ball reached the other end of the lake and disappeared out of sight.

"That's where the river flows out," said Danni. "Sorry – I don't think you'll be getting that ball back."

Frankie glanced at his friends. *We need to get the football back — it's our ticket home!* "Where does the river go?" he said.

"To the sea, eventually," said Danni. "But the track to the football pitches crosses the river downstream. Maybe we can rescue the ball there. Better hurry!"

She led them down a single-track road away from the lake, and the sun dried their clothes as they jogged along. There were a few wooden houses dotted around the landscape, but they didn't see a single other person. Thick forests of tall pine trees carpeted the mountainsides.

"How much further?" asked Charlie, huffing to keep up.

"Nearly there!" said Danni. "There's a short cut." She veered off the road, down a forest path leading into the trees. A sign read "Harlow's Creek".

It was darker beneath the trees, and Frankie found it a bit creepy. He couldn't see more than a few metres ahead.

Soon the trees opened out a little, and they came to a sparkling river surrounded by boulders on either side. A few trees grew over the water, casting it in a dappled light.

"Check this out!" said Charlie. He'd climbed to the top of one of the boulders, tugging on a rope suspended from a tree branch. "It's a rope swing."

Before any of them could say anything, he'd hurled himself off, swooping over the river and landing on the other side. He let go of the rope and it swung back.

"Great," called Frankie. "Now you're stuck on the other side!"

Charlie's face fell. "Oh, I didn't think about that."

"It's all right," said Danni. "All the local kids play here. There's a bridge further downstream. But let's wait

here and see if the football comes past."

They peered out across the water. Frankie felt a gnawing sense of unease. To Danni, the football probably looked like a worthless piece of leather, but to him it was everything.

What if it's gone for good?

CHAPTER 3

After a few minutes, Frankie's heart had sunk to his heels. "This is hopeless!" Charlie shouted from the other side.

Then Max barked.

"There!" said Louise, pointing. Sure enough, the ball was drifting along the river, bouncing over submerged rocks. Frankie felt a flood of relief. Now all they had to do was get it back. But the ball was coming quickly, right in the middle of the current. He scrambled across several rocks and reached out across the water. The ball brushed past his fingertips and kept going.

"After it!" he cried.

They all tore along the river bank together, with Charlie on the opposite side. It was hard going, picking their way over the rocks and tree roots.

"Fetch, Claude!" shouted Danni, and her giant dog leapt into a river pool. For a moment Frankie thought he'd get the ball, but the wave he created pushed the ball further downstream and out of reach.

"Are you sure this is worth it?" called Danni. "It doesn't look like a very good ball anyway."

"Trust me!" said Frankie. "It has a lot of sentimental value." He spotted the narrow wooden bridge up ahead. "There!"

Frankie and Louise sprinted towards it, and Charlie arrived by their side a second or two later.

But as Frankie stood in the centre of the bridge, he knew he couldn't reach down far enough.

"It gets shallower up ahead," said

Danni, racing past the bridge. "The current's more gentle too."

Frankie saw that she was right. The river turned a corner, and a large sandbank split the current in two. He ran off the bridge and followed Danni beneath a cluster of trees.

As they rounded the bend, Charlie gasped. "Oh, wow – look!"

Frankie stopped at his friend's side and a grin spread over his face, despite everything.

Downstream, on a flat piece of sun-baked rock, two bear cubs were rolling around, playing with the magic football. Their fur glistened in the sunlight and their little ears poked up.

"They look like big teddy bears," said Louise.

One of the cubs spotted them, and made a high-pitched wail.

"They don't normally come this close to town," said Danni, a frown creasing her brow.

"What's wrong?" Frankie asked.

"Nothing," she said. "Just — those cubs look very young. If there's a mother around, we should be careful."

Frankie wished he had a camera with him. "Have you got any food?" he asked. "Something to distract them from the football?"

"Yes," said Danni. "But only a banana sandwich." She started to unzip her bag.

"It's OK," Max whispered to Frankie. "I can handle this."

"Max, no!" said Frankie, as his little dog hopped on to a boulder beside the bears. Both were at least twice the size of him.

He barked a few times and, to Frankie's surprise, the bears scrambled away, leaving the ball behind. They darted towards the trees.

Max grabbed the ball in his teeth and turned to them triumphantly, wagging his tail.

"Phew!" said Frankie.

"He's a brave little thing," said Danni.

But then Claude started to bark, the deep sound reverberating. The huge dog backed away.

"Nothing to be scared of," said Max.

The bridge above them creaked

and shuddered a little. Max's tail dropped between his legs.

"Uh-oh," said Charlie.

Frankie looked up. Through the gaps between the timbers of the bridge, he saw an enormous shadow moving slowly. It grew bigger, and bigger, and then ...

"Oh wow," Charlie whispered. "Mr Donald was right. Those things really are huge." As the words left his mouth, the shadow came into view.

"It's ... it's ... it's ..." said Louise. Just this once, she didn't have the right words.

"It's a huge brown bear!" Frankie finished for her.

CHAPTER 4

Frankie's knees felt weak. He couldn't take his eyes off the creature's huge claws and slavering mouth.

Max dropped the ball and whimpered at his ankles.

"What do we do?" whispered Charlie.

"Don't run," said Frankie. "Remember what Mr Donald said. Bears can move fast and climb trees."

The bear suddenly rose up on its hind legs, looming at least two metres tall. It opened its jaws to reveal long yellow teeth. Then it roared, and Frankie was sure he felt the blast of its breath.

"Danni, how about that banana sandwich now?" said Louise.

"Throw it!" said Charlie.

Hands trembling, Danni chucked the sandwich. It landed on the ground in front of the bear. It dropped to all fours again, raking

the ground with its claws. It sniffed
hesitantly, but didn't eat it.

"I guess it doesn't like bananas,"
said Louise.

"Charlie, get on to my shoulders,"
said Frankie.

"Why?" said Charlie.

"We've got to make ourselves
look big," said Frankie. His back
prickled with sweat as he crouched
on the ground. Charlie came up
behind him, and hooked his legs
over Frankie's shoulders. Then
Frankie straightened up, with
Charlie on his back.

This has to work! Frankie thought
desperately.

The bear stared Charlie in the eye. "Come on, come on . . ." Frankie whispered, as he gripped Charlie's legs, feeling his friend swaying on his shoulders. Eventually, the great creature retreated a step.

"You two!" Frankie called. "Quickly! Do the same."

Louise clambered on to Danni's shoulders.

Max, he noticed, was hiding behind Claude.

The bear swung its head left and right, sniffing the air. One of the cubs made a purring sound from below one of the trees, and the

bear growled back. It heaved its body round and slowly walked off the bridge towards its cubs.

Frankie realised he'd been holding his breath all this time. He finally let it out in one big sigh.

"For tourists, you know a lot about bears," said Danni, as she bent down to let Louise climb off her back.

"We learnt about them at school," said Frankie.

Danni took a phone out of her pocket and started to dial. "We're supposed to report bear sightings to the local sheriff."

Frankie glanced at his friends. He

really didn't want the authorities finding out they were here.

"Is that necessary?" he said, grabbing his football. "The bear's gone now."

"Don't worry," said Danni. "The sheriff is my mum!" She grinned. "Hi mum, it's Danni ...."

Frankie waved his friends over while she spoke on the phone.

"We'd better get out of here," he said.

"But what about Danni's football tournament?" asked Charlie.

"If the sheriff comes, she'll ask all sorts of awkward questions," said Frankie.

Louise looked glum. "I guess so ..."

Danni got off the phone. "Good news, guys! My mum's going to come and pick us up in her car. She'll drive us to the game."

Frankie blushed. "I'm really sorry, but we need to leave now," he said.

"Oh ... OK," said Danni, looking sad.

Frankie held his hand out and Danni shook it. Louise and Charlie each gave her a hug. Danni stooped to stroke Max's head.

"Good luck in your tournament," said Louise.

Frankie gripped his ball under

his arm. He and his gang started to walk back the way they'd come. He felt dreadful. Normally the football brought them to help someone. But Danni didn't seem to need their help — at least not now that they'd got rid of the bear.

A voice called out from behind them. "Come on, Claude!" Frankie glanced back. It was Danni, calling to her Newfoundland. The huge dog was following them!

"Go on, big fella," said Max, reaching up to touch noses with his giant friend. "You can't come with us."

Claude whined.

Frankie heard the far-off sounds of wheels on gravel. Then, through the trees, he saw a police car approaching.

"On no!" he said. "We've got to hide."

He broke into a run, and the others followed him into the trees. Under his arm, the magic football

was tingling. Frankie dropped it
to the ground and gave it a kick.
The ball bounced once on the side
of the road, then vanished. In its
place a portal appeared – a disc of
swirling light just hanging in the air.

"Quick!" said Louise. "Danni's
mum is almost here."

Max leapt through first, followed
by Charlie and Louise. Frankie took
a last breath of cool mountain air,
and jumped after them.

CHAPTER 5

Darkness swallowed them up. Frankie panicked. He couldn't see a thing and the air smelled musty.

"Hello?" he said.

"Where are we?" said Louise's voice.

Frankie felt a hand touch his. It

was wearing a glove. "Is that you, Charlie?"

"Yep," said his friend. "Hang on, I've found a wall . . ."

A moment later, bright light made Frankie shield his eyes. They were all standing in a bare room, lined with benches and pegs. Charlie had his hand on the light switch.

"We're in the sports changing room!" Frankie realised.

"It smells horrible!" barked Max.

Frankie glanced down and saw his dog by his feet. "Uh-oh! The football's brought Max back to the

school! But hang on . . . how come
you can still talk?"

Normally the magic football only
gave his dog speech when they
were on their adventures.

"Oh yeah!" said Max. "Pretty
cool, huh?"

Frankie frowned. "Not really!
How are we going to explain this to
mum and dad?"

Max hopped up on the bench.
"Who cares?" he said. "At least now I
can tell them which dog food to buy."

Charlie tried the door, and
thankfully it opened. He peered
out into the corridor. "All clear," he
called back.

"It must still be break time," said Frankie.

Riiiiiing!

"That's the school bell," said Louise. "We'd better get back to class! We'll have to hide Max – somehow."

Frankie scooped up his dog. In the corner of the room he spied the spare kit bin, filled with old sports clothes for when pupils forgot their PE gear. Charlie called it the "B.O. Barrel", because none of the stuff ever got washed.

Max whimpered as Frankie carried him towards it.

"Don't worry, boy," said Frankie.

"I just need something to cover you up."

He fished inside and took out a crumpled football shirt. Max sniffed and his ears flopped down. "Please, not that . . ."

"Only for a while," said Frankie, draping the shirt over his head.

When Frankie and his friends made it back to class everyone else was already in their seats. Including Mr Donald, at the front of the class. He cleared his throat when he saw Frankie.

"Thank you for joining us," he said. His eyes fell on the football shirt in Frankie's hands. "It's not PE today, Frankie."

"I know, sir," said Frankie. "I just remembered I left my kit in the changing room yesterday. I'm going to take it home to have it washed." Carefully, he placed the bundle on top of his schoolbag on the floor. The tip of Max's tail poked out, so Frankie quickly covered it up.

On his desk, he found several books that Mr Donald had been handing out. One had a photo of salmon leaping from a river. Louise sat down and started flicking through the pages.

"We're talking about the Rocky Mountains in the west of Canada," said Mr Donald.

"They're beautiful!" said Charlie. "The air's so clean, the lakes are amazing . . ."

"Yes, they are!" said Mr Donald, looking surprised.

Charlie didn't seem to hear. "And the mountains are massive and capped with snow . . ."

Frankie saw Louise nudge him with her elbow.

"Oh – in the pictures I've seen, anyway," said Charlie.

Mr Donald went on to explain how the mountains had been

formed millions of years ago, making a chain 3,000 miles long. Frankie found his mind drifting back to the *real* Rockies, and Danni. He wondered if she'd told her mum about meeting three English kids and a dog. The sheriff's department would probably try to find them and he felt guilty for running away like they had. Hopefully, though, Danni would get to her tournament on time.

"So, Frankie," said their teacher. "What do you think?"

Frankie sat bolt upright. "Pardon, sir?"

Mr Donald frowned. "It's not like

you to be so distracted," he said. "Is everything all right?"

Frankie forced himself to smile. "Just thinking about football, sir," he said. "Sorry."

Their classmate Kobe raised his hand. "Sir, can I use the toilet please?"

"Of course," said Mr Donald.

After Kobe had left, Mr Donald put some slides up on the projector showing how the ice from the Arctic Circle spread south into Canada during the winter. He began to talk to them about the Inuit tribes who lived in temperatures as low as minus 30 degrees. Just thinking about it made Frankie shiver.

Suddenly the door burst open and Kobe ran back in. His eyes were wide, and his finger trembled as he pointed back towards the corridor.

"S ... S ... Sir!" he said.

"What is it, Kobe?" asked Mr Donald.

Muttering broke out across the desks. Frankie had a sinking feeling.

"I saw an animal!" said Kobe. "Just outside the changing rooms. I think ... I think it was a bear!"

Mr Donald burst out laughing. "Very funny, Kobe," he said. "Now back to your seat, please. We're talking about the Inuit people. Did you know, they have more than fifty different words for snow?"

Then Frankie heard a terrible low growl. The whole class went quiet, including Mr Donald. He dropped his board pen.

In the silence that followed, a shuffling sound came from right outside the classroom door.

"It sounds like footsteps," said a girl called Hannah.

A snorting breath made everyone jump out of their seats. Frankie rushed to the classroom door and peered out through the glass panel. He couldn't see anything at

first – just the empty corridor. Then his eyes caught a shadow moving across the wall near the main school doors, which were open. It slipped away, and the doors closed silently behind it.

Frankie turned to see the class all staring right at him.

"Kobe's right!" he said.

Louise's skin was pale. Charlie buried his face in his gloves.

Frankie swallowed hard. This was bad. *Really* bad.

What have we done? Frankie thought.

PART TWO

CHAPTER 1

"What have we done?" Louise whispered.

The rest of the class sat in silence. With every second that passed, Louise felt more and more desperate. The magic football had always taken them to strange places, and they'd met all sorts of people. But it had never brought anyone back – let alone a dangerous animal!

"Are you certain you saw a bear, Frankie?" asked Mr Donald, gulping.

"I think so," said Frankie. Louise had never seen her friend look so worried. Not even when they'd been two-nil down at half-time against Oak Ridge Primary.

Riiiing! Riiiing! Riiing!

The school bell went off and everyone looked at each other in confusion.

Strange, thought Louise. *The lesson's only just started . . .*

The classroom speakers came on with a crackle, and the headmistress's voice filled the classroom.

"Will all staff please bring their students to the main hall," said the headmistress, her voice trembling. "We have reports of a wild animal on the school premises."

Mr Donald stared at the classroom speakers in astonishment, then shook his head quickly. "OK, class. You heard what the headmistress said. Everyone form an orderly line at the classroom door. Pretend it's a fire drill."

Chairs scraped back and

muttering broke out as Louise's classmates climbed to their feet.

"Maybe the bear escaped from the zoo!" said Hannah.

Mr Donald shrugged. "I suppose it must have, but there aren't any zoos near here," he said. "I'm sure it's a false alarm."

Louise nudged Frankie. "The magic portal must have stayed open," she muttered under her breath. "That must be why Max can still speak, too. Weird, I didn't see the bear following us."

"I suppose we're lucky in a way," said Charlie. "At least the bear didn't catch us in Canada!"

Frankie groaned. "I don't call this lucky!" he said. "We need to find that bear and get it home. Somehow."

Louise remembered the towering creature and shuddered. She would be missing her cubs.

Max poked his nose out from Frankie's bag. "Anyone got any food?"

"Now isn't the time!" said Frankie.

"I meant for the bear!" said Max.

"Stay inside," whispered Frankie, scooping up the bag.

They all gathered in a line, and Mr Donald gingerly opened the classroom door. Their teacher edged into the corridor, then beckoned them on. "Follow me!" he whispered.

Lots of other pupils were emerging from their classrooms, looking excited and scared at the same time.

"Roar!" shouted a voice.

Hannah squealed, and Louise spun round to see Frankie's older brother, Kevin. He had his hands raised like claws.

Max growled from inside Frankie's bag.

"What was that?" asked Kevin, narrowing his eyes.

"Nothing," said Louise, standing in front of the bag.

"I'd like to see him face a real bear," said Charlie in her ear.

The different classes all filed into the main hall. Louise came last with Frankie, Charlie and Kevin.

They'd almost reached the door when Frankie's bag started to whine and wriggle. "No, Max!" said Frankie.

But it was too late. The dirty PE shirt fell to the floor and Max leapt out. Louise shot a glance to the hall door, but everyone else was inside.

"I knew it!" said Kevin. "What's he doing in school?"

"I couldn't stay in there a second longer," said Max. "Dogs have noses hundreds of times more sensitive than people, you know?"

Kevin stared. "It's the football, isn't it? You're up to something!"

"Shush!" said Frankie. "Before Mr Donald—"

"Before Mr Donald *what*?" said their teacher, putting his head around the door. When he caught sight of Max, Louise saw his brow crease in confusion. Then he nodded slowly.

"I see we have a culprit!" he said. "A bear indeed! Who does this dog belong to?"

Louise saw Frankie and Kevin look at each other guiltily. Mr Donald thought that Max was the rogue bear!

"Both of you, in my office," said Mr Donald. "You've a lot of explaining to do."

"But sir!" said Louise. "There really *is* a bear!"

Mr Donald waved his hand at her. "Don't be silly, Louise," he said. "The joke's gone too far."

"She's telling the truth," said Charlie.

Mr Donald's face turned crimson. "Don't try my patience, young man."

"You have to listen," said Louise.

"That's enough!" said the teacher. "I want all of you — and that dog — in my office right now."

CHAPTER 2

A short while later, Louise sat with Charlie on one side and Frankie and his brother on the other. Mr Donald had gone to tell the headmistress that it had all been a false alarm. Max lay on the floor next to Mr Donald's desk. In the corridor outside, the pupils were all heading back to their classrooms, laughing. Louise's stomach was doing flips. There was a real bear out there somewhere, and no one would believe them!

Frankie had finished telling his brother about the trip to Canada. Kevin had known about the football's magic for ages, but even he looked shocked.

"You'll have to tell them the truth!" he said.

"You think they'll believe me?" asked Frankie.

"They'll have to if I tell them," muttered Max.

Frankie looked so glum that

Louise put her arm over his shoulder. "It's OK," she said, "but this time it's gone too far."

"It certainly has, young lady," said a voice from the doorway. Mr Donald stood there. He didn't look quite as angry as before, and Louise was glad. She'd never been in trouble before at school.

A phone rang and Mr Donald took his mobile out of his pocket and put it to his ear. "Yes .... Of course ... I'll be there right now ..." He ended the call and stared from face to face. "*Someone* has to explain to the emergency services that it was a false alarm! You lot, wait here." Then he turned and marched out of the room.

"They'll take the magic football away, won't they?" said Charlie, after a long pause.

Frankie nodded. He still had his bag with him, and he took out the ball, rolling it in his hands. "I guess we had fun while it lasted," he said.

Louise had never seen her friend so defeated. It wasn't like Frankie at all. They'd come up against the odds so many times, but with him leading the team they'd always pulled together. As she thought of all their victories, a spark ignited in her heart.

"It's not over yet," she said. Max gave a yip of approval.

"Isn't it?" said Charlie, staring at his goalie gloves.

Louise grinned. "You heard what Mr Donald said – he'll be back in ten minutes. I reckon we've got nine minutes to find that bear and get it home."

"You can't be serious!" said Kevin.

But Frankie stood up slowly and Charlie sprang to his feet as well, clapping his gloves together.

"Listen, Kev," said Frankie. "I know we don't always get on, but if Donaldo gets back early, please don't tell him anything."

"So what *am* I supposed to say?" asked Kevin.

Max trotted to the door. "Tell him I ran off and they had to find me," he said.

They left Mr Donald's office and darted along the corridor. "I saw it go out the main entrance," said Frankie. He had the football under his arm.

Luckily all the other pupils were back in their classrooms, so the corridor was empty. When they reached the main doors, they swished open. The sun was shining brightly, and Louise had to shield her eyes. She had no idea how they'd be able to capture the bear, but they had to try.

Max lifted his snout. "I smell something this way," he said, scampering off between the school building and the library cabin. Frankie went after him, with Charlie and Louise following.

Max had slowed, nose to the ground, when they reached the sports field. Frankie gasped. "Look!" he said, pointing at the grass.

There, in the muddy ground, were several huge footprints. "The bear!" said Charlie.

Max made a strange snorting

sound. "I don't know – it doesn't smell quite right, but it might just be that horrible sweaty sports shirt messing with my nostrils still."

"They lead this way," said Frankie, setting off again.

The prints led across the football pitch towards a fenced-off area where the school rubbish and recycling bins were kept.

"It's probably looking for scraps of food," said Frankie, his voice hushed.

Louise glanced back at the school. How long would it be before Mr Donald came back to his office and found them gone? And could they really trust Kevin not to tell?

At the fence, they stopped. The paw prints ran through the open gate and into the bin area. Louise could hear something shuffling around on the other side.

Frankie tiptoed towards the

gate, and with every step, Louise expected the rampaging bear to come hurtling through.

But it didn't. Frankie managed to get the gate handle and pull it closed. The bear was trapped inside!

"Now what?" said Charlie.

Louise listened. She couldn't hear anything any more. *That's weird*, she thought. *Why isn't the bear trying to escape?*

She looked again at the prints on the ground, and felt a smile spreading across her lips.

"Of course!" she muttered. "Why didn't I see it before?"

"What?" said Frankie and Charlie at the same time.

Louise went past Frankie and grabbed the gate handle, ready to pull it open.

"What are you doing?" said Charlie.

"Look at those markings," she said. "It's got four claw-pads."

"So?" said Frankie.

"A bear has five," said Louise. "I read it in one of the books Mr Donald gave us."

"So maybe this bear lost a toe?" said Charlie.

Louise shook her head and flung the gate wide open.

Frankie and Charlie leapt backwards as Claude the Newfoundland came bounding out. He knocked Louise over and licked her face happily.

"Or maybe," said Louise, "this isn't a bear at all!"

CHAPTER 3

Everyone gathered round and patted and stroked Claude. Max ran excitedly in circles.

"Hey, big guy!" he said. "I knew you didn't smell like a bear!"

Claude gave two deep woofs, tongue lolling.

"Danni will be really worried,"

said Frankie. "You know what this means?"

"Are we going to miss lunch?" said Charlie.

"Of course we are!" said Louise. "We've got to get Claude back to Canada!"

"We'll use the puddle," said Frankie. "The football already did it once, so it should work again."

They all ran back towards the school, with Claude jogging along beside them. His huge paws sounded like a horse's pounding hooves. Louise's shoes and trousers were filthy from the mud, but she didn't care. All that mattered now was getting Claude home.

But as they reached the puddle at the edge of the car park, Frankie skidded to a halt.

"Oh no!" he said.

Louise saw why – the puddle had gone! She looked up at the sun glaring down. Now wasn't the time to give her friends a lecture on the water cycle. "It's dried up," she said, despairing.

Frankie took his football and dropped it on the place where the puddle had been. Nothing happened.

"Try another," said Charlie, pointing further along the path.

They ran to the next puddle, which was still there — just.

Frankie dropped the football. It splashed, but no portal appeared.

"What now?" he said. "We can't get back to Canada."

Claude cocked his head, his eyes drooping sadly.

"Don't worry," said Max. "We'll find a way."

Louise's mind whirled. *We need something Canadian for the football's magic to work.* She looked around desperately.

But she couldn't see anything that might help. The sun was shining, a light wind was blowing,

and the leaves in the trees were
rustling. And then the idea clicked
into place.

"I know!" she said. "Leaves! The
maple tree!"

Frankie grinned and clicked his
fingers. "By the sports pavilion!"

They all set off again, and
Louise's heart filled with hope.

They stumbled to a halt beside the tall tree. She'd never noticed its distinctive leaves before, but Mr Donald was right – they were just like the one on the Canadian flag.

"Here goes!" said Frankie.

He kicked the ball hard at the trunk. Louise drew a sharp breath as the ball disappeared into the bark, leaving behind a shimmering doorway. It had worked!

"Bye, Claude," said Charlie, patting the dog on the head with his glove. "Have a safe trip home."

Claude didn't budge.

"Go on!" said Frankie, pointing. "Home's that way!"

The Newfie backed away.

"He's scared," said Max. "Come on, big fella. In you go."

Claude still wasn't moving.

"One of us will have to go with him," said Frankie. "I volunteer."

"I'm coming too!" said Louise. Secretly, she wanted to see Danni again.

Charlie sighed. "No lunch for me, then. I can't let you go alone."

Together they approached the tree, with Max leading the way. Claude trotted after them.

Louise saw Frankie disappear into the tree, his body swallowed up by the swirling light. As she stepped after him, the school grounds vanished from her sight, and she felt her body sucked away by a magical force. It was like being whipped around in a hurricane, and everything was a blur.

Just as suddenly, she felt her feet on the ground.

Louise blinked to clear her vision. She was standing next to a cabin, where people were queuing up for hot drinks. On the other side of the building were several five-a-side football pitches. Frankie and Charlie looked as confused as Louise felt.

Then, Claude barked loudly.

"Claude?" said a voice.

The queue of people broke apart, and on the other side, sitting on a bench beside one of the pitches, was Danni in her football kit. Claude bounded through the gap. Danni was drinking from a water bottle, but opened her arms as the huge dog went galloping towards her. She met him with an embrace.

"Oh, thank goodness!" said a woman standing nearby with a steaming mug. She was wearing a grey uniform and a wide-brimmed hat. Louise saw a metal badge pinned to her chest.

That must be Danni's mum, she realised.

A moment later, Danni came rushing towards them with Claude at her side. When she saw Louise and her friends, she clapped her hands in delight.

"You found Claude!" she said. "Mum, these are the friends I told you about."

The sheriff looked at them. "Well, hi there," she said with a warm smile. "Danni tells me you're on holiday with your folks. Quite an exciting time you're having, I guess?"

"Yes!" said Frankie. "But really,

we'd better be going. Just wanted to make sure you got your dog back."

"No, stay!" said Danni. "My team is in the final. The game's going to start in five minutes."

Frankie looked uncertain, but Louise realised that all of the people in the crowd — and Danni's mum — were watching them. It would be impossible to just slip away.

"OK," she said. "We'll stay and watch."

"Great!" said Danni. "I need to go and have a team talk. Thanks again for finding Claude."

After Danni had run off back to her team, and her mum was looking after Claude, Louise huddled with her friends.

"What about Mr D?" said Charlie. "He's going to go supernova if we don't get back to his office."

Louise nodded. "Let's wait until the game starts. That will be the best chance to sneak off. Everyone will have their eyes on the game."

"Good thinking," said Frankie. He looked worried, though.

"What's the matter?" she asked.

Frankie bit his lip. "Normally the football wants us to help someone," he said, "but this time we haven't. It was our fault that Claude got lost in the first place."

"Maybe the football made a mistake," said Max at their ankles.

Just then, Danni came over. She looked close to tears, and pulled off her gloves. "You may as well leave now," she said. "The game's off."

"What? Why?" said Louise.

"My team-mate Erica can't carry on," said Danni. "She's got a stomach bug and she's been bravely playing through it until now. We haven't got a sub, so we're out of the tournament!"

Louise saw out of the corner of

her eye that Frankie was grinning. "No, you're not," he said. "I know a great sub."

"Who could fill in at such short notice?" said Danni. "The game starts in three minutes!"

Charlie, Frankie and Max all looked at Louise.

"Me?" said Louise, a thrill of excitement running through her.

"Can you play football?" asked Danni.

Charlie laughed. "Do bears like honey?"

Could I . . . could I really play in a Canadian tournament? she asked herself. But they'd been brought here to help someone, hadn't they? Frankie had just said that himself.

"I'll do it!" she cried.

CHAPTER 4

Butterflies fluttered in Louise's
stomach as she got changed,
surrounded by girls who were all
older than her. As well as Danni,
there was Melissa, Carly and Tash.
Could she really hold her own in
this team? She'd had to borrow a
spare kit, and the red shirt was a

bit big. But as Louise pulled on a pair of trainers, the nerves lifted a little. Mr Donald always said it was normal to be nervous in the build-up to a big game. Even Frankie admitted he sometimes felt a bit unsure of himself before important matches.

"Ready?" said Danni. Louise nodded. "Don't worry," said the older girl. "Just do your best."

They jogged out of the changing room together, and Louise saw all the girls' parents and friends standing on the sidelines, waiting and cheering. The opposite team, wearing blue, were already on the pitch knocking a ball between them. They were all *massive*!

"Go, Lou!" called a voice above all the others. She searched the crowd and saw Frankie standing with Charlie and Max. Nearby, Claude was sitting patiently beside Danni's mum.

I can't let them all down, thought Louise.

Danni had explained that the game was ten minutes long with no half-time break. The blue team had won the tournament the last two years running!

Danni took her place in goal, while Louise ran to the middle of the pitch to face her opponent, a stocky girl with brown plaits. She held out her hand. "I'm Louise," she said. The other girl didn't smile, but she took Louise's hand and squeezed it hard. "I'm Clem," she replied.

The ref blew the whistle and dropped the ball between them.

Clem lashed out her foot and kicked Louise in the shin. But the ref hadn't seen! Louise hopped, clutching her leg as the other team got the ball and started passing towards goal. Louise ran off the pain and backtracked.

This is a bad start! she thought.

Luckily, one of Danni's defenders made a tackle, and suddenly the ball was coming back to Louise's feet. She did a clever turn past a blue player, and in a few strides was bearing down on the goal. *Stay calm*, she told herself. *Just pretend you're playing with Frankie in the park.*

"Oof!" A blue shape ploughed into Louise's shoulder, sending her tumbling across the ground without the ball.

"Foul!" she heard Charlie cry.

Clem was grinning. "Just a little shoulder barge," she said.

"Fine," said Louise through gritted teeth. She got up and dusted herself down. She'd played physical matches before. This was no different. The important thing was not to lose her temper.

The game restarted and Louise did her best to stay out of Clem's way. The rest of the blue team weren't much better, though.

Wherever Louise turned, one of them was marking her, often kicking at her ankles or trailing a foot to trip her up. Because they were so much bigger, they used their weight to shove her off the ball. And once, when she was almost ready to head in a goal, she felt her shirt being tugged so hard she fell over.

The girl called Tash helped her up. "You're doing great," she said.

"Really?" said Louise.

"Sure," said Melissa, running past. "While it's still nil-nil we have a chance, right? And only a minute left!"

A minute! thought Louise. She'd been concentrating so hard on the game, time had flown by.

It's only nil-nil because of how well Danni is doing in goal, thought Louise. Their new friend was an amazing keeper. Whereas Charlie moved around the goal like a cannonball, his feet and hands a blur, Danni managed to spread her long limbs and make herself look huge. Her movements were smooth and precise, leaping to cover every corner of her goal.

The blue keeper kicked the ball out, and Carly jumped to head it. She didn't quite reach and the ball skimmed off to one of the opposition. Louise sprinted back as Melissa tried to make a tackle. The blue player chipped the ball to Clem. Louise put herself between the ball and the goal.

"Out of my way," said Clem, her feet stepping over the ball quickly. Louise kept her eye on it, ready to make the tackle, then lunged in. Clem tapped the ball with the outside of her foot to the left, into her team-mate's path. Louise looked round in horror as the player and Danni both ran at the ball from opposite sides. Who would get there first?

As the blue player prepared to shoot, Danni hurled herself headlong at the ball on the ground. Louise grimaced as they met the ball at almost the same moment — boots and gloves colliding.

"Argh!" cried Danni, curling up in pain. The blue player flew over the top of her, rolling along the ground. The ref blew his whistle.

"Penalty!" he said, pointing towards the spot. Half the crowd booed, and the other half cheered.

"No way was that a foul!" shouted Frankie from the sidelines. "Danni got there first."

Louise ran with the rest of the

team to where Danni lay on the ground, cradling her hand. Her face was twisted with pain.

"Are you OK?" asked Carly.

Danni shook her head. "It's my wrist. Sorry, guys. I thought I got the ball first."

"You did!" said Melissa. "It shouldn't have been a penalty."

The ref peered over them. "Can you carry on?" he said.

"She's hurt her wrist," said Louise.

"Do you have any subs?" he asked.

"No," said Tash.

The ref tapped his watch. "You can have a one-minute time-out," he said. "Then you either have to play, or forfeit the match."

As he walked away, Frankie came rushing on to the pitch.

"That looked painful!" said Frankie.

Wincing, Danni stood up.

"You can't play on!" said Melissa. "You're injured."

Danni flexed her fingers and grinned. "It's fine," she said, but Louise could see the pain on her face.

"Are you sure?" she asked.

Danni nodded and glared up the pitch at the team in blue. "We're not giving up," she said firmly.

"Non-players off the pitch, please!" said the ref.

Danni began to walk back towards the goal, and Clem stepped forward with the ball and placed it on the penalty spot. "Never mind," she said. "At least the best team won."

"Wait!" said Charlie, who was behind the goal.

"Thirty seconds until we re-start," said the ref.

Louise joined Danni and Charlie by the goal.

"Don't try and stop me," said Danni.

"It's not that," said Charlie. "I

want to help you. I want you to wear these."

He looked at his hands, then carefully pulled off first one glove, then the other. Louise couldn't believe what she was seeing. Charlie *never* took off his gloves. Not when he ate, not when he had a bath, not even when he slept. His hands were so pale!

"Thanks!" said Danni. "But I've got my own gloves."

"Not like these," said Charlie. "They're magic." He and Louise shared a glance.

"You should wear them," said

Louise quickly. "He doesn't remove his gloves for anybody!"

Danni looked uncertain, but she eventually nodded. "I'll need all the help I can get," she said. In a few seconds she'd taken off her gloves and put on Charlie's.

"Good luck!" Louise said, as her new friend took her place between the goalposts.

CHAPTER 5

The whole crowd was silent as
Clem stepped back from the
football.

Louise saw Frankie and Charlie
with their hands over their mouths
on the sidelines. Danni's mum had
her sheriff's hat clutched to her
chest. There could only be about

twenty seconds of the match to
go.

One of the blue team came up
behind Louise. "You guys are toast.
Clem's never missed a penalty."

"We'll see," said Louise.

The ref blew his whistle and
Clem started her run up. Danni bent
her knees in goal. Louise held her
breath.

Clem struck the ball, and it
streaked towards the bottom
corner of the net. Danni went into
a dive. *She won't make it!* thought
Louise. Clem was already lifting
her hands in the air. But at the last
moment, Danni's arm stretched out

in a flash. Her fingertips brushed
the ball. It collided with the post
and bounced off.

The crowd cheered, and Clem's
arms dropped to her side. "What?"
she gasped. Louise had her eyes on
the ball.

"Let's finish this!" she said.

Melissa sprang after the ball and got there just before a blue player. She dribbled past her opponent. Louise was already running into an open space. Melissa kicked a hard pass to Tash. But one of Clem's team ran into her. Tash managed to hold her ground. Then she chipped the ball over another player's head to Carly. Carly headed it on to Louise.

"Do it, Lou!" called Charlie. "Score!"

This time Louise knew to watch out for Clem. The older girl was bearing down, an angry look on her face. Louise ran towards the goal with the ball at her feet. But at the last possible moment – just before she was flattened by Clem – she stopped dead in her tracks and pulled the ball back with her foot.

"What are you doing?" cried Clem as she careered past, unable to stop. She skidded and fell flat on her face.

The blue goalkeeper spread her arms, her feet widely spaced. Louise couldn't see a way past.

Unless . . .

She turned her body as though she was about to release a powerful shot. The keeper's eyes widened.

Louise swung her foot, but instead of using her instep, she side-footed the ball softly. It rolled right between the keeper's legs and into the net. Half a second later the whistle went.

"Noooo!" yelled Clem.

"Supergoal!" cried Frankie.

Louise turned to see all her

players running towards her, Danni included. They all gathered round in a team hug. "We did it!" Danni said. "We beat them!"

Louise felt her face glowing with pride. On the sidelines, Max was jumping up and down and even Claude was wagging his tail.

As they broke apart, Louise felt a hand on her shoulder. She saw it was Clem. The older girl held out a hand. "Well played," she said.

Louise looked at the hand uncertainly.

"I mean it," Clem added. "That was an amazing goal. You guys deserved to win."

Louise shook her hand, then those of the rest of the blue team. Now the game was over, they were all really nice.

As they walked off the pitch together, Charlie patted Louise on the back. "I knew you could do it!" he said.

"Thanks, guys," said Louise.

"I'd love to stay and celebrate," said Frankie, "but maybe we ought to get going!" He pointed to the football under his arm, which was glowing slightly. It was ready to travel home.

"Shouldn't we say goodbye to Danni?" said Charlie.

"And Claude!" said Max.

Louise looked around, but she couldn't see their new friend anywhere, or her dog. "No, let's go," she said sadly. "We can sneak back round the cabin when no one's watching."

Leaving all the players and spectators behind, they went back to the spot where the portal had left them. Frankie placed the ball on the ground.

"I'm glad the football brought us here," he said. "What an adventure!"

Someone cleared their throat, and Louise spun around. Danni was watching them with an ice-pack on her wrist.

"What do you mean, the football *brought* you here?" she asked.

Frankie's mouth started opening and closing, but he obviously didn't know what to say.

"Would you believe it if we told you it was magic?" asked Louise.

"No," said Danni. "Of course not."

Louise stepped forward and kicked the ball at the cabin. A portal of swirling light appeared where it struck the wall.

"Oh!" said Danni, stepping back. "That's not possible!"

"We have to go," said Frankie. "Please don't tell anyone."

Danni blinked. "They wouldn't believe me anyway," she whispered.

Louise heard more footsteps and her heart sped up. *We're going to be found out!*

But it was only Claude. The huge dog shambled around the side of the cabin. He had something in his jaws, which he dropped to the ground in front of Danni.

"My gloves!" said Charlie. "I can't believe I almost forgot them."

Danni picked them up and handed them to Charlie. "Let me guess. They're magic, too!" she said. "Just like Frankie's football. I feel bad now — isn't that cheating?"

Charlie pulled them on and shook his head. "Actually, they aren't magic," he said. "I just told you that to help you believe in yourself."

"Phew!" said Danni. She knelt down and stroked Max. "Will I ever see you guys again?"

"Maybe," said Frankie, approaching the portal. "You and Lou might meet in the Women's World Cup one day!"

"I hope so!" said Louise. She waved as she stepped into the portal beside her friends. "Bye, Danni. Bye, Claude."

"Bye every ..." Danni began.

Her words were cut off and Louise found herself back in the school car park. She saw Mr Donald standing by the main doors, his arms folded.

"What are you all doing out here?" he called over. Louise gulped as he walked across to them, shaking his head. He stared at Frankie. "Your brother told me your naughty dog ran off again." He hesitated. "So I'll let you off this time. But no more false alarms, please." He spotted a boy kicking a ball against the school wall and frowned. "Excuse me, I have things to do," he said, marching away.

Louise smiled at her friends. "You know what this means, don't you?" she asked.

Frankie nodded, his eyes wide. "Kevin covered for us," he said.

Charlie gave a low whistle. "This day is full of strange events," he said.

Louise turned around in a circle, looking for their little dog friend. "Where *is* Max?" she said.

"He's going home," Frankie said, pointing towards the school gates. Louise saw Frankie's mum standing there, holding up Max's lead. She must have come looking for him.

"We should get to class," Louise said.

As they walked back towards the school, Frankie tossed his ball up and caught it. "You know what, I feel *I* could teach a lesson about Canada!"

They all laughed as they walked through the doors. They had helped someone after all — and Louise had enjoyed the best game of her life!

ACKNOWLEDGEMENTS

[illegible faded text]

ACKNOWLEDGEMENTS

Many thanks to everyone at
Hachette Children's Group; Neil
Blair, Zoe King, Daniel Teweles
and all at The Blair Partnership;
Luella Wright for bringing my
characters to life; special thanks to
Michael Ford for all his wisdom and
patience; and to Steve Kutner for

being a great friend and for all his help and guidance, not just with the book but with everything.

**Turn the page for an
exclusive extract
from Frankie's next
adventure,
Meteor Madness,
coming soon!**

Frankie, Louise, Charlie and Max
are on holiday together, and want
to visit the theme park in the
holiday camp. But park is closed
due to an electrical fault, and
none of the rides have any power.
Frankie and his friends start
playing a game of football instead,

but when the ball goes over the fence in to the theme park they sneak in to get it back . . .

All was still apart from some coloured lights flashing further into the park. Frankie's skin tingled. Had the power come back on? Or was this the work of the magic football? It wouldn't be the first time it had made strange things happen.

Most of the rides were silent. He saw a roller coaster, a clown's circus, a ghost house and several others. The flashing lights were coming from a model space shuttle supported by a long beam. Frankie guessed it swung up and down. The ride was called "Galaxy Quest!"

But he couldn't see the ball anywhere.

Max trotted up to the spaceship and sniffed around. Then he rested his paws on it.

"I think he's smelled something," said Frankie. Leaning over the spaceship's edge, he saw the ball lodged under one of the seats. "It's here!" Frankie jumped up into the spaceship.

"Cool!" said Charlie, climbing up as well. "I've always wanted to be an astronaut! One small save for man, one giant save for—"

He went quiet as the ride creaked into motion, swinging slowly forwards on the long arm with a creak. Frankie lost his balance and stumbled backwards on to one of the seats.

"Er ... is it supposed to do that?" said Louise. "Maybe I should go and get someone."

The ride rocked backwards again. Frankie saw the ball was glowing a little.

"I think it's the magic of the football!" he said. "It must want us to go and help someone. Quick, climb in!"

Louise grabbed Max and passed

him to Frankie as the spaceship
swung back and forth, then
scrambled in herself. "Fasten your
seatbelts!" she cried.

The ride moved faster, swinging
high into the air. Frankie's stomach
yo-yoed up and down, but he
pulled down the harness bars over
his head until they clicked into
place. He held Max in his lap.

"Do you think it's safe?" Charlie
shouted.

"I trust the football!" said
Frankie, as the shuttle rocked
higher.

The spaceship swooped
downwards, then climbed up the

other side. This time it didn't stop and swung upside-down, before plummeting again. "It's getting faster!" shouted Louise.

The forest and the other rides shot past as the spaceship dipped and rose in huge circles. Frankie wondered if he'd made a mistake. What if the ride was malfunctioning?

He saw smoke coming from the arm that held the rocket.

"We've got to get off!" cried Charlie.

Sparks fizzed in all directions. Then, with a few pops, the bolts and screws exploded. The whole ride began to shake. "It's falling to bits!" yelled Louise. Max was trembling on Frankie's knee, and he held him tight. They spun faster and faster until everything was a blur.

Then as the rocket rose again, Frankie felt it lurch and heard a horrible tear of metal.

Frankie closed his eyes as they shot into the sky.

FRANKIE'S MAGIC FOOTBALL
WEBSITE

Have you had a chance to check out
frankiesmagicfootball.co.uk yet?

Get involved in **competitions**, find out **news** and
updates about the series, play **games** and watch
videos featuring the author, **Frank Lampard!**

Visit the site to join
Frankie's FC today!

COMING SOON!

*Frankie's Magic Football
Sticker Activity Book*

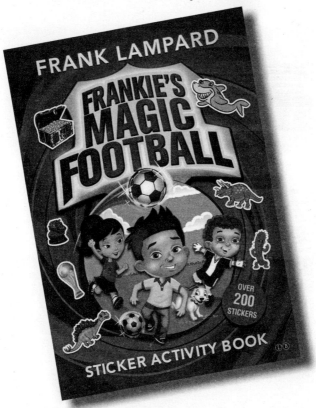

With over 200 stickers!

Have you read these Frankie's Magic Football adventures?

Have you read these Frankie's Magic Football adventures?